The Chain of Giving

Hiawyn Oram
Illustrated by Richard Johnson

Chapters

The Brothers Have a Plan

Tembi and Zeb lived in a little village in Africa. It had not rained there for a long, long time.

"What are we going to do, Brother Zeb?" cried Tembi. "We have had no rain for so long. Nothing will grow and there's no food to eat. Everyone in the village is hungry!"

"Yes, Brother Tembi," agreed Zeb. "We are all hungry, but don't worry. I know what we can do. I have some rice seed. We can sow the seed and watch it grow. Then there will be food for everyone!"

"But Brother Zeb," said Tembi. "If there is no rain, how will the seed grow?"

"We'll set out and look for a place near a lake," explained Zeb. "It will be wet there. That's where we'll sow the seed."

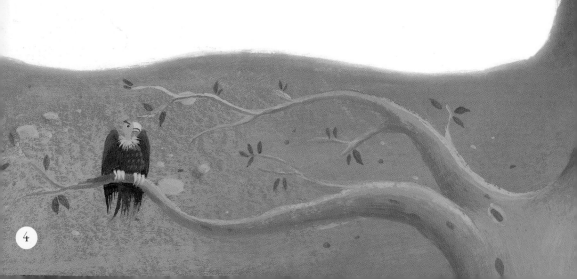

Goose Eats the Seed!

So the brothers set out to look for a lake. They looked for many days. Then at last, Zeb saw a lake. "Hey, Brother Tembi! A lake!" he cried. "This is where we will sow the seed and watch it grow!"

The brothers worked hard all day. As soon as they were finished, they fell fast asleep. But as they slept, Goose flew overhead. She saw the seed and swooped down. "Seed! Seed! Seed! How I love seed!" honked Goose as she ate. Goose ate all the seed!

Later, the brothers woke up and saw Goose. "Hey, Goose!" cried Zeb. "You have eaten all our seed! And that seed was going to grow into rice!"

"And that rice was going to feed our village!" shouted Tembi. "Now you have eaten our seed, we have no food at all!"

"I am very sorry I ate the seed," honked
Goose. "I will make it up to you – I promise!
I have laid my eggs under Tree. Soon they will
hatch and there will be geese. I'll give you the
geese and they will lay eggs to feed your village."

"Thank you, Goose," said the brothers.
"That is very good of you. We will wait for
your geese."

Tree Loses His Flowers

But later that day, a strong wind blew in. The wind blew Tree from side to side. All at once, the wind blew so hard that one of Tree's branches blew down. The branch fell on Goose's eggs!

"Smashed! Smashed!" honked Goose. "All my eggs have been smashed! Now there will be no geese to lay eggs to feed the village. What will the brothers do now?"

"I am sorry, Goose," said Tree. "I am sorry, brothers. It was my branch that smashed the eggs, so I will make it up to you. Look! I have flowers. They will soon be cotton and I will give you the cotton to sell. Then you can buy food to feed your village."

"Thank you, Tree," said Tembi. "That is very good of you. We will wait for your cotton."

Old Elephant's Tusks

But later that day, Old Elephant came and ate all of Tree's flowers! "Yum! Yum! How I love flowers! Yum! Yum! Yum!" hooted Old Elephant.

"Stop, Old Elephant! Stop!" shouted Zeb.

"Stop! Stop!" cried Tree. "My flowers are not for you! They are for the brothers!"

"I am sorry, Tree," said Old Elephant. "I am sorry, brothers. I ate the flowers, so I will make it up to you. Look! I have these tusks. They are very old and soon they will fall out. I will give you my tusks to sell. Then you can buy food to feed your village."

"Thank you, Old Elephant," said the brothers. "That is very good of you. We will wait for your tusks."

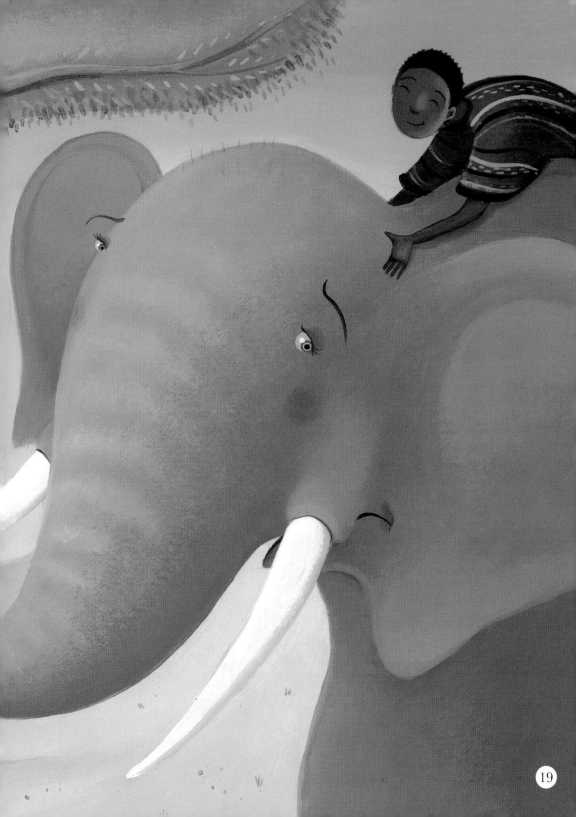

White Ants to the Rescue

But later, Old Elephant went down to the river and tried to cross the bridge. White Ants had been eating away at the bridge and when Old Elephant tried to cross the bridge, it broke. Old Elephant fell in the river!

"White Ants! White Ants!" hooted Old Elephant. "What have you done? Because you ate away at the bridge, I fell in the river. Because I fell in the river, my tusks fell out. Because the river is flowing fast, it took away my tusks. Now there are no tusks for the boys to sell to buy food to feed their village! What will we do?"

"We are sorry, Old Elephant," said the White
Ants. "We are sorry, brothers. We ate away at
the bridge, so we will make it up to you."

"But what can little ants do to help?" said
Old Elephant.

"We can help!" cried the White Ants. "We
know where the mushrooms grow. We'll get
the mushroom seeds and take them to the
village. Mushrooms grow very fast and when
it rains, there will be mushrooms for everyone
in the village!"

So the White Ants took the mushroom seeds
to the village. The next day it rained and the
mushrooms grew fast. Soon, there was food for
everyone in the village.

"You see, Brother Tembi," said Zeb. "There
is now food for everyone!"

"Yes, Brother Zeb," said Tembi. "We have
saved the village with the help of Goose, Tree,
Old Elephant and some very clever White Ants!"